Red Deception

By

J.C. Murtagh

To my lifelong best friends, Amber and Michelle.
Thank you for being my biggest fans
and always believing in me.

Acknowledgements

I want to thank my editor, Charity Heller, from the Mighty Pen who made this book shine with her editing expertise.

Chapter 1

Tears of anger ran down Judith's grimy cheeks. She swallowed the searing pain that burned her left cheek then turned her attention to the horizon, where the sun crested the foggy mountains to the east.

Tracing her finger over the dusty windowpane, she fell transfixed on Blacwin manor, which crowned the dark pines in the distance.

"Judith!" called her mother-in-law, Gertrude. "Are you still up there?"

The question made Judith seethe. Reluctantly, she turned away from the window and looked around the pitifully small loft space where she slept each night with her husband and son. A broken trunk and a hay bed were the only furnishings in the room.

She climbed down the ladder to the room below and found Gertrude sweeping up ash from the previous night's fire.

She glared at Judith from across the soot-clouded room.

"Did you do what I told you?" she asked, wiping her hands on her apron.

"I had planned to wash the floors when you finish sweeping."

Fear seized Judith's heart as two meaty hands grasped her shoulders from behind.

"Get out of my way!" her father-in-law Bart, bellowed, and shoved her into the nearest wall.

The foul stench of his breath clouded Judith's lungs and she covered her head, anticipating another strike.

Her tender cheek was a burning reminder of his last assault on her that morning for letting two eggs roll off the counter while she was preparing the morning meal.

He stalked past her like a rabid bear and grabbed the pitcher of warm ale off the counter. She refrained from grimacing as the pale liquid dribbled down his chin into his flea-infested beard.

"Fetch some water, Judith. The floor isn't going to wash itself," her mother-in-law said.

Judith walked to the front door and pushed it open, relishing the warm sunlight that greeted her. She grabbed the bucket on the doorstep and looked up to see her son running toward her with a fist full of fresh flowers.

"Mummy!" he cried, his mess of blond hair bouncing with every step.

"What have you got there, Sam?" she asked with a smile.

"Wildflowers!"

Her husband Garreth followed behind him, carrying an axe over his shoulder.

"Go show your grand-mum, and she will put them in some water," Judith urged, sending her rosy-cheeked son past her.

"Where are you off to?" Garreth asked once he was toe to toe with her.

"To fetch some water to wash the floor," Judith answered, clinging to the bucket handle with both hands.

"Make sure there isn't a toad in it this time. My father nearly removed your head."

Judith smirked. "I told you before, that was your son's doing."

"I think you did it on purpose. I know you spite my parents, but they mean well."

Judith looked past him, watching a swarm of flies buzz around the pigsty.

He took her shoulder. "I know this is not the life I promised, but we have no other choice, Judith. One day I will rebuild us our own home."

The same story, just a different day, Judith thought.

He kissed her cheek. "I promise you."

She brushed past him. "I need to fetch the water."

Judith took the longer route through the woods. She swung the bucket with each step and closed her eyes. The birds' chirping combined with the whistling wind, put her mind at ease. She ignored the mud that sucked at the bottom of her thin boots and splashed her tawny wool dress.

She found the familiar stream over-flowing due to a recent rainstorm and could not resist visiting her favorite spot near the water, a large boulder at the stream's edge.

She settled on the boulder and leaned over the stream. She cupped her hands, dipped them into the cool water, and rinsed the grime from her face.

She peered down at her reflection in the rippling water and traced her dripping fingertips over her tender cheek, which would likely bruise by nightfall.

Judith often wondered what would have happened if she had never married Garreth Timbolt. She and her parents had been in a dire situation, having neither coin nor food. She had been at the peak of womanhood, ready to become a bride, and they wanted a better life for her.

Garreth, who was fifteen years her senior, welcomed the marriage and promised her a good life. In return, she had to leave behind her family and the village she loved. The memory of her parents weeping as they said their goodbyes still brought her remorse.

Garreth treated her kindly in the beginning and their love for one another bloomed. She would wake with his kiss on her lips every morning and as soon as she found out she was expecting their son, Garreth informed everyone he knew. Two short years after she took Garreth's name, the beautiful cottage he built for them burned to the ground.

The cottage had collapsed onto itself, scattering orange cinders into the cold black night. Moving to Caldwell to live with his parents was their only hope after every possession they had turned to ash…

Her thoughts were interrupted when she noticed a bright red heap lying in the tall grass across the stream. She stood up on the boulder for a better look; perhaps it was a skinned animal left to rot.

Curiosity piqued, she gathered her long dark hair over her shoulder and lifted her dress to make the short leap across the stream.

She approached it with hesitation. As she drew closer, she noticed it was not an animal at all, but a woman lying face down, wearing a red cloak.

Judith clasped her throat and looked around to see if there was any evidence of an attack. Nothing seemed out of place as far as she could see. She circled the female with cautious steps, wondering if she might be asleep.

"Hello?" Judith called.

There was no reply.

She knelt beside the woman and gently pulled the hood of the cloak back to see a sea of thick black hair resembling her own falling over alabaster skin. She realized the woman was not asleep—she was dead.

She squelched a scream and backed away. Her foot brushed a parchment rolled up in the woman's stiff fingers. She removed it and read elegant script as best she could.

Dear Mother and Father,

By the time this reaches you, I will be with God. I warned you that if you should force me to marry Baron Blacwin, I will end my life before I have the chance to meet his cold black eyes or live to suffer his beastly demeanor. Therefore, it shall be. With this poison, I am free.

Your loving daughter,

Lora Noire of Wilshire

Judith read the script several times, her heart aching for the young maiden. She could imagine the despair the girl felt; death's release had crossed her own mind many times.

She had never met Baron Blacwin, but she had heard stories about him.

They said he had hair and eyes that rivaled the darkest night and his face was as sour as his disposition. Tales stated that he transformed into a bat at night and flew around Caldwell village, attacking merchants who were not honest with their shillings.

My own life is much worse than this prim maiden's was, Judith thought. *I would be honored to marry the baron. All of my problems would be just a memory.*

Her fingers traced the velvet edge of the blood-red cloak, and her gaze moved over the girl's mess of raven hair.

She looks so much like me. I wonder if we could be mistaken for one another. Judith mused.

She reprimanded herself for thinking such a thought. She knew she should alert someone and cease her useless daydreaming.

She stood up to head for the village, but her attention again wandered back to the lifeless corpse.

She touched own cheek, re-living the moment her father-in-law's thick palm hit her so hard she saw flickers of light. *Could I be Lora Noire? If only for a day...?*

Her heart began to race as she looked around the quiet clearing. Without another moment of hesitation, she rushed back to the body of Lora Noire and knelt beside her.

"Forgive me, my lady," she whispered as her trembling hands undressed the corpse.

Within moments, she had traded her itchy wool dress for Lora's beautiful red gown and matching velvet cloak. The dress fit her snugly on her bosom and waist, but it would have to do.

Checking her appearance in the stream water, Judith could barely believe her eyes. She was transformed from a poor peasant to a lady.

She wasted no time redressing Lora's corpse in her own faded rags and dragging her away from the clearing.

She left the body in the shaded woods, beneath a tall pine. She swallowed her guilt, posed Lora's hands over her abdomen, and tucked some wildflowers into her stiff fingers. The ensemble was complete.

If she looked quickly enough, Judith swore she could see herself laying there.

A chill coursed through her, and she fled out of the woods into the sunlight.

Just as she pulled the hood of her cloak up, a voice call out behind her.

"Lady Noire!"

She turned around to see a man striding towards her through the tall grass.

She pulled the cloak down further over her head and lowered her gaze to the ground.

"My lady, we have been searching for you all morning! Where have you been? Did that moment of fresh air you needed turn into a stroll in the wood?"

Judith could barely hear the question over the sound of her own heart beating in her ears. She nodded, staring at the ground.

"Come along. The baron is waiting. We do not want to keep him. They say he has a nasty temper."

The man put his frail hand on shoulder and led her away from the stream toward the road. A beautiful carriage with two grey horses awaited them. The carriage door swung open for her, and the driver assisted her inside. She took her seat to the right, and the man who had found her in the woods sat across from her.

She peeked out from below her hood to watch him remove a cloth from his pocket and dab sweat from his balding head, mottled from age.

The carriage lurched forward suddenly, causing her to almost fall off the seat. She squealed and clung to the window curtain.

The man stared at her with a perplexed expression. "Are you well, Lady Noire?"

She nodded, afraid to speak in fear she might give herself away. She forced her fingers to release the silk curtain before she tore it down.

"I know your upset about the arrangement. Your father just wants what is best for you."

Judith kept her silence, clinging to the seat in unease.

"Lady Noire, your hands are filthy. Whatever were you doing?"

Judith glanced down at her palms coated in grime and shrugged in response.

"It would be best if you clean them before we reach the manor."

He held out the cloth to her.

She hesitated before taking it and rubbing the dirt from her palms and fingers.

"Your hands look swollen," he noted.

She knew her hands were fuller than Lora's were.

She ignored his comment, keeping her head bowed as she worked the dirt out from between her fingers. She could scarcely believe where she was and what she was doing.

She tried to stop her hands from trembling but it was no use. What would she say if she was discovered? Her rash decision had her stomach twisted as tight as a rope. She knew when she did not return to the cottage they would look for her. The thought of Sam worrying for her nauseated her with guilt, but it was too late to turn back...

Once finished, she handed the cloth back.

He took it and tossed it out the carriage window.

"You are certain you're fine? You have not said two words since I found you."

She nodded.

"Very well." He groaned and leaned back on the seat. "Wake me when we arrive. Searching for you all morning has left me worn."

She folded her hands in her lap, glad to be free of his inquisition. Not another word was shared between them rest of the ride.

Chapter 2

It was dusk when the carriage came to a halt. Judith peeked out of the carriage window, where a perfect view of the baron's grey stone manor greeted her.

It was a breath taking sight. So many nights she had watched this ominous manor from her own little window, its roof tops illuminated in moonlight, its flickering windows beckoning her.

The carriage door swung open and the driver's hand guided her out.

Judith could see the orange flicker of hearth light in every window. Two somber guards with dark stares awaited their arrival at the gate. Each held a gold-tipped spear in his left hand.

The man whom she had ridden with spoke for them. "This is Lady Lora Noire of Wilshire, and I am Lyle Barnsby, a hired hand of the Noire family."

"Welcome to Blacwin Manor," the guard on the left replied, and the iron gates opened to welcome them inside.

The manor grew more intimidating as they passed between two gargoyle statues. Judith did not question Lora Noire's apprehension any longer. A thought occurred to her: Had Lora and Baron Blacwin met before?

"Have I met Baron Blacwin?" she asked Lyle.

He paused. "I am not certain. You cannot recall if you have met him?"

"I cannot."

"I am sure you would recall his presence if you two had met. It would be frightfully embarrassing if you have forgotten your meeting."

Her steps became hesitated, but he urged her along with a hand on her shoulder. The thick summer air became harder to breathe with every step she took toward the immense oak doors that felt like a monsters maw, waiting to swallow her.

A female servant came out to greet them.

"Good evening, and welcome to Blacwin manor. You must be Lady Noire. We have been expecting you."

Judith simply bowed her head, choked with fear.

Lyle cleared his throat. "Yes, this is Lady Lora Noire. You must excuse her manners; the ride has left her worn. I am Lyle Barnsby, her hired hand for the journey. She has some trunks on the carriage, if you would be so kind as to assist us in bringing them to her room."

"Yes, of course. We will have someone to fetch them right away. Lady Noire, let me take your cloak," she offered, holding out her hands.

"No," Judith said, pulling the red cloak around her shoulders and stepping out of reach.

"My Lady Noire, what has gotten into you?" Lyle questioned.

"I would like to leave my cloak on, please. I am afraid I may have caught a chill."

"A chill? We should get her to her room immediately. A change of clothes will do her good," Lyle said.

"Of course," the servant said. "Come along, Lady Noire. We have a hearth burning in your guest room."

"Lady Noire, I will give your regards to your father," Lyle called from the doorway as she was led into the dark manor.

He disappeared behind the tall manor doors.

Judith's heart hammered in her ears as she was led through the foreboding manor. Thick drapes covered most of the windows, shunning any light of day. Paintings lined the walls with gruesome figures that watched her with cold stares as if they knew her secret. She balled the cloak into her fists and closed her eyes, listening to her echoed her footfalls on the elegant marble floors that made the manor feel more like a mausoleum. She finally arrived in an empty feast hall.

An elegant long table that could seat at least thirty guests sat in the center of the room. At the far end of the hall, a hearth beckoned them with warmth, its face decorated with weaponry. Taxidermy trophies of all species imaginable stared down at her from every wall. Elaborate tapestries told stories of hunts, feasting, and war.

"Are you hungry, Lady Noire? We have prepared a supper in your name. Do you wish for some warm cider to remove your chill?"

"No, thank you."

"Very well. This way to your room."

They paused before large double doors carved with mirrored images of stags rearing up. The servant led her through another series of sinister corridors and up a flight of winding stairs.

She produced a key from the pocket of her dress and unlocked the door. Warmth rushed out to greet them. Judith could not wipe the look of awe from her face as she stared at the most immaculate room she had ever seen. A fire burned in the hearth, as promised. An immense dark wood four-poster canopy bed loomed in the far corner. The bedding looked soft and wonderful, made of red damask silk reserved for royalty.

"May I take your cloak now, Lady Noire?"

Judith untied the cloak, let it slip from her shoulders, and crossed her arms, feeling as if the truth of her identity were written all over her.

"Is there anything more I can do for you, Lady Noire?" the servant asked.

"No, thank you," Judith replied, stepping further into the room, admiring the sheer size of it.

"I will leave you to rest, then. We will fetch you for supper."

Judith waited until the doors closed before she walked to the bed and brushed her fingertips over the luxurious linens. The coverlet was double-stitched to keep the cold out on a winter night. A black bear hide lay folded at the foot of the bed for extra warmth. Tears of joy burned Judith's eyes. The room was truly something out of a dream.

Like a child, she threw herself down on the fluffed pillows and nuzzled her face into them. Giggling, she kicked off her muddy boots and rubbed her feet against the bearskin blanket.

A knock on the door scared the joy right out of her.

She leapt off the bed and straightened her dress.

"Yes?" she called.

"Lady Noire? I have your belongings." a man's voice called back.

She pulled open the door to see a pock-faced man standing beside a stack of trunks.

The man greeted her with a tip of his head. "May I enter?"

"Yes," Judith stepped aside.

She settled on the edge of the bed and watched the sweat roll down the man's flushed brow as he stacked the trunks neatly in the corner.

"Enjoy your evening," he offered before departing.

I most definitely will... Judith thought, smiling at the trunks.

She waited until his footsteps disappeared before investigating the trunks contents. She opened the first one and lifted out a lavish purple dress only a baroness could afford. Laying it aside, she picked up the next. The dresses were never ending, an array of colors from marigold to forest green. After she had laid them out all over the bed, she realized she needed to choose one for supper. After inner debate on whether red made her look too sultry, she chose the forest green because it brought out the green in her hazel eyes.

She finished exploring two more trunks of Lora's belongings before she came across her grooming supplies. She found a silver hairbrush and matching hand mirror.

She brushed her hair until it shone.

Two servants joined her in her room shortly after. One milled about, putting away the contents of the trunk, while the other helped her into a warm bath. After the bath, they assisted her into the emerald dress. Judith felt like royalty as she stared at her reflection in the mirror. The dress was a snug fit on her hips and breasts and was just a bit short on her, just like Lora's dress she had worn earlier. They gathered her long black hair into a hair net with emerald gems that matched her dress then placed Lora's silk slippers on her feet.

Once she was ready, the servants led her downstairs. Before Judith even set foot inside the hall, her stomach rumbled from the enticing aroma of freshly roasted meat. The large doors of the hall opened, and she was escorted inside.

He stood at the head of the table dressed in his fabled black attire, from his doublet to his boots. His straight black hair fell past his shoulders. An elegant silver rapier with an elaborate jeweled hilt dangled from his belt.

Once she met his onyx stare, she knew there was no question about why he was the most feared man in Caldwell.

She curtsied and bowed her head.

"Welcome to Blacwin manor, Lady Noire."

His voice was deep and condescending.

"Thank you, Baron Blacwin," she said, hoping he did not hear the trepidation in her voice.

He held out his hand to her.

She felt speechless as she placed her hand in his, and did her best not to tremble.

"It is my honor to have you as a guest."

"There is no place I'd rather be," she replied.

His lips parted in an amused chortle. "Not many have said that. You *have* heard the rumors about me, haven't you?"

Judith's cheeks burned. "I do not judge a man on a play of words."

Their gazes met again, and Judith felt a strange prickling in her belly as his dark eyes burrowed into her with serious intent.

"Your father's letters of your beauty hardly do you justice."

She smiled, having never heard kind words about her beauty before. "You are too kind."

"Shall we sit?"

Judith nodded and followed him to the head of the table.

She took a seat at the baron's right.

"Will we be dining alone?" she asked, noting the table was only set for two.

"Yes. I thought we might grow to know one another. Is that suitable to you?"

"Yes."

"Did you find your room satisfactory?" he picked up his wine goblet and his eyes wandered over her cleavage that was nearly bursting from her dress.

Judith's face seared again. "It's the most elegant room I have ever seen."

The baron received his supper plate. Her mouth watered at the sight of the honey-glazed hen and fresh vegetables that were placed before each of them. She had never seen a meal so grand. She waited for the baron to begin eating before she took even one bite. She had never tasted anything so flavorful. She had to pace herself, so as not to finish her meal before he did.

"Is it true I have been sent here for a marriage arrangement?" she asked.

"That is correct."

"Have you been married before?"

He lowered his silverware and his gaze hardened. "Yes, once. She was sickly and barren. She died from a fever."

"You have my condolences."

He responded with frown and turned his attention back to his supper. He did not have much to say after that, and they ate in silence.

Following the hens, they were served large slabs of pork drizzled with cranberry sauce, and blood pudding for dessert.

Judith drank three glasses of the sweetest wine she had ever tasted during the meal, and afterwards she was feeling confident enough to accept the baron's offer to the manor.

She rested her hand on the curve of his arm as he led her around the grounds, talking of his duties while showing her the old chapel, granary, dairy barn, buttery, pantry, servant's hold, and finally the solar, his very own chamber.

She was surprised when he welcomed her inside.

A magnificent granite hearth blazed at the farthest wall, surrounded by arched stained glass windows. She imagined he had the most luxurious room in the entire kingdom.

A tall bed with four posts twisted like unicorn's horns held rein over the room, which was dressed in forest-green velvet. Thick fur rugs were strewn about the room, warding off the cold from the marble floor. A tall wardrobe sat alone in the corner and two plush chairs rested before the hearth. Judith thought the room matched his personality perfectly.

"Tell me, Lora," he said, pausing before the hearth with his back to her, "did you come to my manor willingly, or is this your father's wish?"

The question caught Judith off guard. She pulled at the sides of her dress, pretending to smooth it. "It was my choice. I was pleased to be taken into consideration."

She watched his head tilt slightly to the left; hearth light glowed along his chiseled jaw and revealed a slight smile.

"There is no need for dishonesty. I know my reputation. No one comes to visit my manor any more, unless by force or by duty."

Judith swallowed. "Well, I am pleased to be here, Baron Blacwin."

"You may call me Cal in private. Calvin Blacwin is my name."

He took up two crystal chalices and filled each with dark wine. He handed one to her, and she brushed her fingers over the crystal. She had never held a glass so luxurious.

For a moment, there was only the sound of firewood snapping in the hearth and the whistling of the wind outside.

She brought the chalice to her lips and tasted the wine. It was sweeter than the glasses she had enjoyed at dinner.

He followed her example and took a drink, letting his gaze linger on hers. "As young as you are, you have a woman's shape. I find it very becoming."

"Well, I am nearing my nineteenth year."

His voice changed from silk to concern. "Your father said you just celebrated your sixteenth year."

Judith inwardly cursed herself and forced a soft laugh. "Oh, there is no fooling you, Lord Blacwin."

"No there isn't," he answered, squinting.

She hid her apprehension with a long sip of wine.

Once they finished their wine, he set their chalices aside.

"Do you know what your eyes tell me?" he asked as he drew her to him, resting his hand on her waist.

She could feel warmth of his palm permeating through the dress.

Her words caught in her throat as she met his gaze. "No. What do they tell you?"

"That you have a secret."

Judith tried to pull away, but his other hand came to rest on her upper back.

"I have no secrets," she said, looking over at the stained glass window.

"No?" he insisted, dipping his head to get her attention.

"No," she answered again, looking into his eyes. She wondered if he could hear how hard her heart was beating.

"Well, I have a secret."

"Do you?"

She could smell the rich wine on his breath.

"Yes. I have not kissed another woman since my wife passed six winters ago. Tonight is the first time I desire to."

She flushed at his revelation.

"Will you do me the honor?"

"Yes," she answered softly.

Before she could prepare, his warm lips pressed against hers.

Heat flowed from her neck to her legs. She had never been kissed with such passion. Her hand grasped at the back of his doublet and she leaned into him.

His hold on her tightened, and wrapped her in an embrace. Their tongues brushed once and the kiss ended. She rested her forehead against his shoulder, feeling weak.

His lips brushed against her temple. "Would you stay the night with me, if only as innocent company?"

She swallowed hard, his kiss still lingering on her lips. "I would."

She felt his smile without seeing it.

"If you wish to change into your night clothes, I understand."

"I should, yes," she said, feeling suddenly intoxicated.

He released her. "I will be waiting here."

Judith stumbled over her own feet as she left the solar and hurried back to her room. She closed the doors, pressed her back against them, and laughed. Her mind was clouded with lust and excitement. When she put on Lora Noire's dress, she never expected she would be seducing the Baron of Caldwell.

What made it even worse was her enjoyment of this whole affair. She could not wait to feel his warm hands and his inviting lips on her again.

She rushed to the bed, where a beautiful carmine red robe with snowshoe trim had been laid out for her. She wasted no time undressing and slipping the elegant fabric over her naked body.

Suddenly, her mind was plagued with thoughts of Garreth: he promised her nice things, much like this. There was a time when Garreth's touch warmed her, but since they moved to Caldwell, all she felt were cold calloused hands when he touched her. The night that their cottage went up in flames, so did their marriage. She felt alive when the baron kissed her and that was something she never thought she would feel again.

She buried her guilt and tied the robe around her waist. Discarding the bejeweled hair net, she let her hair spill over her shoulders and brushed it smooth. She checked her appearance in the mirror, feeling more like a baroness by the moment. Content with her appearance, she returned to the Baron's solar and knocked softly on the door.

"It is open," he called from within.

She stepped inside to find he had also changed into a charcoal grey night robe. He sat in one of the plush chairs before the hearth, with a glass of wine.

He rose to his feet and looked her over. "That robe is breathtaking on you."

"Oh, this?" she rubbed her hands over the snowshoe neckline. "It was a gift from some other suitor who wanted my hand. My mother insisted I bring it with me."

He ran his fingers over her waist. "Didn't your mother pass some time ago?"

"She did?"

"Your father said so, unless he was deceiving me."

She blinked. "She did pass away. She died, yes. She was dear to my heart. I always refer to her like she is still here."

"I see. A mother is irreplaceable. You have my condolences," he said taking her hand.

"Thank you," she said avoiding his eyes.

He led her over to the stained-glass windows near the hearth. Rain droplets trickled down the brightly colored panes like tears.

"This room once belonged to my mother. She had these stained glass windows put in...she always said this manor needed color. Every time I see the sun come through them, I think of her."

"They are beautiful, the centerpiece of the room."

He took up her hand, and his warm lips covered her knuckles, "Much like you."

She gave a soft smile.

"Do you desire to be a mother someday, Lora?"

"Of course I do, but there is no rush."

"If you decide to be the baroness of Caldwell, we will have someone to care for our children, wet nurses to suckle them, tend to them...all you would have to do is give them life."

"That sounds wonderful, but would you love me if I grew wide and plump from giving you children?"

He smiled. "I'd love every child you gave me, and the womb in which you carried them, no matter the size."

She giggled. "That is easy to assume."

She reached down to cover it, but his hand captured hers. She glanced up into his dark eyes, and he planted a kiss on her lips that made her toes curl.

He led her over to the bed and sat her down at its edge. She felt a gust of cool air on her lower leg and found it exposed.

"Tell me, Lora, have you spent time with any other men?"

"Some, but none as handsome as you, Baron Blacwin," she said, combing her hand through his hair.

"Cal," he corrected.

"Cal."

He seemed pleased to hear saying his name. "May I inquire how well you became acquainted?"

She sucked on her lower lip and stared into the hearth. "A kiss here and there...and I allowed one to touch my unmentionables."

She felt the heat coming off him as he sat beside her.

"Where exactly did he touch you?" he asked, looking over at her with ravenous eyes.

Her cheeks burned as she took his hand and placed it over her left breast. "Here."

His adam's apple bobbed.

"And...?"

She brushed his fingertips over her midriff. "And here."

His fingers tickled her as they inched lower between her naval and pelvic bone. "And here?"

"Yes..." she whispered, closing her eyes.

His breathing deepened as his hand brushed over her pelvic bone. "Here as well?"

"Mm...yes..." she whispered, her body aching for more of his touch.

His hand slipped away, and before she could protest, he dropped to one knee and stared into her eyes.

"Would you allow me to please you as I see fit?"

His proposition sent a burst of warmth rushing through her. "I would."

She felt light-headed as he pulled her robe open and exposed her to the open air. She wrapped her legs around his shoulders as his tongue delighted her wet center. She cried out in pleasure, raking her fingers through his silken hair as she came to a finish shortly after he began.

She fell back on the bed and he climbed over her, looking like a wolf about to ravish its prey. She removed his black doublet and their tongues met in slow, tender brushes that made her burn with desire.

She did not hesitate when he parted her trembling thighs; his breath on her neck was warm and intoxicating.

"How much of you would you allow me to have, Lora?" he asked, rubbing his palms over her parted thighs.

"I'd allow you whatever you wish," she whispered. She had never felt such desire.

"Even your innocence?"

Her innocence? She was by no means a virgin but the baron obviously assumed Lora was. She would have to play the part.

"If you desire it," she answered cautiously, hoping he did.

"I do. But if you give yourself to me, I would have to marry you. I do not believe in taking the innocence of a young woman and discarding her. Would you oblige to becoming my wife?"

"I would," she answered without hesitation.

His dark eyes burned into hers. "Then it shall be."

She could see her own reflection in his eyes, and she looked like the young maiden she claimed to be: Lora Noire, all for his taking.

She feigned pain when he entered her for the sake of her virginal status, but by the end of their lovemaking, she had cried out in pleasure so often she was hoarse.

She had never experienced anything so wonderful. Their lovemaking continued into the early morning hours, until they were both too exhausted to go on and fell asleep entwined one another's arms.

Chapter 3

She sat up in bed, her heart racing as confusion set in. A blush warmed her cheeks as she recalled her night with Baron Blacwin. Pulling the soft blankets up to her neck, she glanced over at the stained-glass window where warm sunlight spilled into the room, leaving a mosaic of vibrant colors on the marble floor.

Birds called to one another from the trees outside the window. It was a perfect morning.

Baron Blacwin entered the solar carrying a tray of tea. He smiled finding her still abed.

"Good morning," he said, setting a cup of tea on the bedside table for her.

"Morning," Judith replied, rubbing her hand through her untidy hair.

He settled at the foot of the bed. "I trust you slept well."

"I did, thank you."

He rubbed his hand over her covered leg and watched her sip her tea. "I hope I was not too forceful with you last night."

"No, you were a perfect gentleman," she assured him.

He stepped over to her bedside and planted a kiss on her lips. "It was the best night I ever had with a woman."

"There will be many more to come, I hope," she said, smiling over her teacup.

He paused and his satisfied look faded into concern.

"Is something wrong?"

"Your face...it is bruised," he said, brushing his thumb over her cheekbone. "How did this happen?"

"Oh." She blushed and turned her face away. "It is nothing."

"You must tell me," he insisted. "Did someone strike you?"

She looked into his eyes, so full of concern. "I fell."

"You fell?" he drew her chin up so her gaze met his. "Do not be afraid to tell me the truth, Lora. No one will hurt you here. Was it your father?"

Judith opened her mouth to answer, but a knock on the door interrupted her.

The baron rose to his feet to greet the unexpected guest. "You may enter."

A servant stepped in and bowed. "Good day, Baron Blacwin."

"What is it?" he demanded.

"We checked on Lady Noire this morning, but she was not in her room." The old man's gaze moved over to her, and his puckered face became pink. "Oh, there you are, Lady Noire. My greatest apologies."

"Yes, she is with me. Now, if you are through interrupting us..."

"Forgive me for the intrusion."

"Before you go, let it be known that she has accepted my marriage proposal and a date has not been set."

His words made her body throb with anxiety. She almost forgot that promise she made in lust.

"Congratulations. Shall I send out a formal announcement?"

"Not now. We will see to it later."

"Forgive my interruption once again. Enjoy your morning." The servant backed out of the room and closed the door.

The baron turned back to Judith, who wore an apprehensive look on her face.

"Do you have an appetite?"

"No, I am still full from our supper."

"I know much has transpired since you arrived last evening. Are you having second thoughts about our arrangement?"

"No, of course not."

He took her hand and kissed her knuckles. "Good. I would be miserable if you changed your mind."

His stare fell on her bruised cheek again.

"I should go dress. I've been abed all morning."

He helped her into her robe and turned her to face him. "Will you meet me when you are finished? I'd like you to assist me with the announcement."

"Yes, I will meet you in the hall."

He leaned in and kissed her brow before releasing her.

She hurried to the door, brushing a hand over her hair.

"Lora," he called before she could escape.

"Yes?"

He strode over to her and lifted her chin with his fingertip. Chills ran over her as his dark eyes burrowed into her. "You are my betrothed now—we will have no secrets."

She knew what he meant. He wanted an explanation for her bruise.

"I understand."

That was not the answer he wanted. "I want to discuss it later."

"We will, I promise."

He seemed pleased with her answer and let her go.

She hurried to her room and closed the heavy doors behind her. Leaning back against them, she felt the weight of her lies upon her.

What have you done, Judith? Her mind chastised her. In just a day she had lied to countless faces, lured the most powerful man into marriage thus breaking her previous marriage vows, and putting her life at risk.

Every moment that passed, she became more tangled in her web of deception. Tears burned her eyelids. She wondered, just how much longer would she be able to play the part of Lora Noire?

She entered the hall later that morning to see the baron sitting at the head of the table. He rose and pulled out her seat for her. A servant poured her a fresh cup of tea.

After they were both seated, Baron Blacwin took a pastry from the tray between them. Any other time, Judith would have gladly nibbled one of the sweet rolls, but that morning, she had not the stomach for it.

"That dress is astonishing on you," he said.

She glanced down at the maroon and gold dress she had picked for the day. It fit her better than the others she tried on. "Thank you."

She grabbed a butter cookie from the tray and he took her hand beneath the table. Just as she placed the sweet cookie between her lips, the baron's messenger came into the hall.

He bowed before them both. "Baron Blacwin, Lady Noire, I have interesting news from town."

Baron Blacwin leaned back in his seat. "What is it Roger?"

The messenger rubbed the top of his beak shaped nose. "A girl was found dead in the woods."

Judith lowered her gaze to the cookie in her hand, afraid to breathe.

"Dead? What was the cause?" the baron asked.

"There has been no word on the cause. At first, the hunters that found her thought she was asleep, but upon further examination, it was discovered that she is indeed dead. They believe she is a peasant who lives on the edge of town."

Judith tried to swallow her bite of cookie, but her throat closed up and she choked.

Both men looked toward her with concern.

She sipped her tea and patted her chest. "Forgive me."

Once the baron saw she was fine, he looked back at Roger.

"We should pay our respects."

"I'd advise waiting a day." the messenger said. "They are not certain who she is. I will keep you alert to any news."

The baron nodded and finished his tea.

"Well, in the meantime, Lora and I will take a ride to the outskirts of the manor. I want her to see the whole manor grounds."

Judith looked at him, unsure she liked that idea. "I have only ridden once. My father did not want me riding for fear I would get thrown."

"My steed is gentle. I will make sure no harm comes to you. We will ride together."

Judith reluctantly rose and took the baron's hand. They left the manor and followed the cobble path toward the stables. Judith could barely contain her anxiety as she imagined the villagers finding Lora's corpse in the woods. Her husband would recognize her dead or alive for sure. The thought of her lie unraveling any moment caused her to groan aloud.

"Lora? Are you well?"

"Yes, just a bit weary from last night," she answered.

"That is normal," he said and led her into the stable. Judith waited near the doors, while the baron walked over to the stable hand that had just finished dressing his black courser.

Blacwin lifted himself into the saddle, cantered over to her, and offered his hand. She climbed up into the saddle behind him and they rode out toward the open field behind the manor.

It was a beautiful summer day. Flocks of birds hiding in the tall grasses scattered into the skies when they came to close.

A half hour's ride from the manor, the baron stopped and dismounted.

"What are we doing?" Judith asked as she slid from the saddle into his arms.

"I thought we would come out here and spend some time alone. It is a nice and peaceful day, don't you agree?"

Judith looked around admiring the view of tall pines lining the field. The manor stood like a beacon on the horizon. "Yes, it's beautiful."

He took her hand and looked into her eyes.

"You captivate me like no other woman, Lora."

She blushed. "Thank you."

"Tell me the truth. Are you having second thoughts on our marriage arrangement? Do you think it's too soon?"

"No," she answered quickly.

"We will have to notify your father; no doubt he will be pleased."

That however, she doubted.

There was no doubt once Lora's father laid his eyes on her he would know she was not his daughter.

She drew in a deep breath and pulled away from him, looking up at the manor on the hill. "We do not have to send word to him just yet. Let us wait and spend more time together."

"Why?"

"He is ill tempered. He may think something is amiss."

"He sent you here in hopes of a marriage proposal, did he not?"

"Yes, but… I still wish to wait."

She stared off toward the thicket of trees, resisting the urge to flee.

He took her by the arm and turned her to face him. "You fear him, don't you?"

"Don't be ridiculous."

"Every time I mention him you look away from me or make an excuse. You're hiding something."

"I am not."

"He left the mark on your face, didn't he?"

"It's nothing, I told you I fell." She turned her face away, her cheeks burning with guilt.

"Once you are Baroness of Caldwell, no one will ever hurt you again Lora. I promise you that."

Judith's eyes filled with tears. "I am not worthy of being your baroness."

"You are every bit worthy. No one will disagree." He drew her into him and kissed her.

She wrapped her arms around him and returned his kiss wanting nothing more than to live in this fantasy forever.

"I know it has only been a day, but I believe I'm falling in love with you," he whispered placing a soft kiss on her forehead.

She rested her cheek against his shoulder. "I feel the same way, Cal."

His kisses moved down over her nose and met her lips. She returned his kisses with uninhibited passion, letting her tongue delve deep into his mouth.

His fingers worked loose the lace on her bodice that held her breasts taught.

The same burning urgency for him as the night before came rushing back.

"Cal," she whispered as he covered her cleavage with heated kisses.

"I must have you again," he whispered, slipping her dress down her shoulders and baring her breasts.

She removed her dress completely, and he settled in the grass and drew her on top of him. Straddling his lap, she enjoyed the feeling as he savored her breasts, causing her to cry out with reckless abandon. She would never forget the way he felt making love to her there in the open field, with the sun on her face and the wild grass tickling her thighs. The cool breeze could not temper the heat between them.

The sun was low in the sky by the time they had spent themselves of one another. She lay against his chest, listening to quiet hum of the evening as day settled into night.

"Do you ever wish you could remain in a moment for all eternity?" she asked, combing her fingers through cool grass.

"Yes. I wish to remain here, in this moment," he answered with a content sigh.

She lifted her head and looked into his eyes. "Me too."

He brushed her hair away from her cheek. "We will share many of these moments, Lora."

She closed her eyes as he traced her lips with his finger.

"You're gentle heart has changed me. You have given me a reason to smile again."

"We barely know each other. Your feelings may change," she answered.

"Why would you think so?"

"I could be deceiving you. I could be marrying you just for the status of being a baroness," she said laying her head down on shoulder.

"I have been deceived often enough to know, and besides, if you were planning on doing that, you wouldn't have told me."

She closed her eyes as a pang of guilt stabbed at her. "I suppose you're right."

He kissed the top of her head. "I am."

They returned to the manor just before supper. She excused herself to her room to freshen up. A tub of water was brought to her to her for bathing.

While she relaxed in the water, she daydreamed of what it would be like to truly be Blacwin's baroness, never to clean another dish, sweep another hearth, or cook another meal. It was all too good to be true.

No matter how much she wanted it, she knew she could never be Lora Noire Baroness of Caldwell. The truth was, she was a lowborn peasant ad could never be accepted as anything more.

She dressed and entered the dining hall to see the baron and his messenger, Roger, speaking again.

They both looked over at her.

She held her breath and curtsied. "Evening."

The baron excused his messenger and walked over to greet her.

"Is everything well?" she asked as he took her hands in his.

"Yes," he said, kissing her knuckles. "How was your bath?"

"Relaxing," she answered, feeling her worry seep away.

"Good."

He led her to her seat where they enjoyed the first course of roasted wild boar and fresh vegetables followed by a bean and wild rice soup.

Just as they were being served fresh fruit tarts for dessert, Roger returned soaked from the evening rain.

He bowed before the table. "My lord and lady, I hate to interrupt but I have important news."

Judith clutched her dress beneath the table.

"Yes?" Blacwin asked.

"Lady Noire's father has heard the news and wishes to congratulate you."

Blacwin looked over at Judith.

"Word travels fast. Very well, will he be sending a gift?" he asked Roger.

"Yes," the messenger replied. "In fact he is in route to the manor as we speak to present you with the gift himself. He should be arriving tomorrow at noon."

Judith felt the soup she just enjoyed rise into her throat.

"What?" she asked in disbelief. "You cannot be serious!"

Roger's brow creased. "It is true. He asked me to notify you both. He is very pleased."

"Is he?" Judith gulped down some wine to hide her distress.

Blacwin reached beneath the table to take her hand. "Very well. We will accommodate him."

"Oh, and I have news of the woman who was found dead in the forest. The family to whom it was thought she belonged, did not know who she was."

Baron Blacwin arched a brow.

Judith closed her eyes.

"What is more peculiar," the messenger continued, "is that the Timbolt family is indeed missing a girl who looks almost identical to this dead woman. They claim the dead woman is even wearing the dress girl was last seen in."

Judith felt as if the stone ceiling was crumbling down on her. Fear had her in a chokehold. All she could do was listen helplessly.

"They are sure it is not the missing girl? Corpses can look very different from the living."

The messenger shrugged. "They say nay."

Judith gagged and pressed her fingertips against her lips.

Blacwin glanced at Judith for her opinion. "Lora, you look pale. Are you well?"

"Actually I am not... I should lie down," she said, rising to her feet.

Blacwin stood and watched her with concern. "Shall I assist you to your room?"

"No, I can manage."

"Shall I send someone to examine you?"

Judith just shook her head and walked from the hall without another word, feeling panic surging through her.

I must escape, but where do I go? Her mind cried.

She began to run toward her room, her legs threatening to give out on her.

Once they find out I am not truly Lora, will they think I took her life? Would the baron hear my plea of innocence or would he throw me in a dark dungeon cell for the rest of my life?

In safety of her chamber, she locked the doors behind her. The room became a blur as she crumbled to the ground and burst into a teary fit. She missed her son, and even her husband. She wished she never put on Lora's red dress. She wished she could turn back time. She prayed for forgiveness, but she knew not even prayer could save her...it never did.

Hours passed. She sobbed, paced and cursed, but no sound solution came to her. Insane thoughts danced through her mind, killing herself, killing her husband, killing Lora's father. Her only sound choices were to tell the truth, or run.

She yearned to tell the baron the truth, but every time she went to do it, she turned away from the door in fear of what he might say.

She remained alone for most the evening, and a knock finally erupted on the door. She did not have to ask who it was. She sat before the flickering hearth, feeling emotionally numb.

"Come in," she answered.

Blacwin tried opening the door, but it was locked. "Lora? Are you well?"

She pinched the bridge of her nose and willed herself to answer. "Yes."

"Will you be joining me in the solar tonight?"

"Not tonight," she answered as a fresh tear slipped from the corner of her eye."

"Open the door. I must see you."

"I am resting."

"Lora, it is not a request."

She walked to the door, unlocked it, and let it swing open slowly.

His look of concern caused her eyes to tear up again.

"You're crying…"

He reached out to touch her cheek.

She turned her face away. "Please, don't. I don't want you to see me like this."

"It's because your father is coming isn't it?" He stepped inside the room and closed the door. "If you two are truly so bitter I will not welcome him."

"It doesn't matter," she sobbed, watching the flames dance in the hearth.

"Lora, there is more to this than you are telling me."

She grimaced with her back turned to him. "I cannot tell you."

"Why? You do not trust me with your secrets?"

"Of course I do!" She yelled, wishing she could just confess.

"Then what is it?"

"You don't know me. He does not know me. No one does."

"What do you mean?"

I am not his daughter you dolt! I am not Lora Noire! She wanted to shout.

"I've not been honest, Cal. I need to think of a way to tell you the truth."

He frowned. "Lora, I will not judge you. Did he force himself upon you?"

"No! Please stop confronting me about him. He did nothing!"

The baron looked confused and released her hand.

"I will be in the hall for my father's arrival, tomorrow. I will tell you afterwards."

"Promise me," he took her hand and kissed the back of it.

Tears threatened to flood her gaze. "Goodnight Cal."

"Promise me."

It took every ounce of resistance not to fall into his arms, sobbing, and tell him the truth. She knew it would not end well. This fantasy, no matter how sweet, was at its end.

"I promise."

He left the room and she covered her face, shaking with more heavy sobs.

Chapter 4

Just before the sun crested the mountains to the east, Judith dressed and crept down the hall to the rear of the manor. She recalled how the stable met the exterior wall. By climbing an old ladder by the stable, she was able to reach the ivy and climbing weeds that snaked over the top of the manor wall. She used them like ropes to her lower herself to the safety of the opposite side.

Her palms burned and bled by the time her feet met the underbrush. She turned around to find herself in the mouth of the peaceful Caldwell forest, a place she once sought comfort, now felt dark and foreboding. She wandered helplessly through the forest, stumbling through the thick trees until she found a path. It was the road to Caldwell. She turned back in the direction of the manor and tears choked her. She would miss him.

As she walked along the road, the dangers of bandits and hungry animals watching her kept her almost as uneasy as going back to Garreth and his parents. Before long, she was standing before the cottage.

No one will ever hurt you again. His voice rang out in her memory. That promise had been made to Lora Noire, not to her.

She grabbed her chest as the door opened suddenly and her husband stood before her, looking as if he had seen a ghost.

She did not know whether to smile or frown. "Garreth."

"Judith, my Judith, you're alive!" He squeezed her against him. "You are truly alive. Thank God! Where have you been?"

She grasped onto him and closed her eyes, unable to speak. Where had she been? The truth sounded too surreal to be believed.

The shrill scream of her son as he came running at her with his arms outstretched interrupted her answer.

"Mummy!"

She knelt and took Sam into her arms. "Sam!"

The thought of the sorrow she put her son through made her heart heavy.

"Mummy, I missed you so much. Are you hurt?" he asked against her ear.

She kissed his dirty cheeks. "No. I am quite all right, Sam."

"Where were you Mummy?"

Looking into her sons innocent eyes made her all the more guilty.

"Lost," she whispered. "I was lost."

Her welcome was short. She sat down to the morning meal and was greeted with a sneer by her father-in-law.

"We thought you had up and died on us. You were probably hiding in the woods this whole time, wanting us to worry, you little witch."

She looked to Garreth, who ignored his father's comment.

"I was lost in the woods."

"Lost." Her mother-in-law snorted. "You're lucky to be alive. I have fallen behind on just about everything without you here, Judith."

"I'm sorry."

"We're out of flour," she complained, ladling some watery pottage into Judith's bowl. "We won't have any bread tonight."

After eating such wonderful food at the manor, the pottage tasted like pig slop.

"How did you get lost, Mummy?" Sam asked, slurping his pottage.

Judith took a deep breath and glanced down at her spoon. "I ran into some bandits."

Garreth lowered his bowl. "Bandits?"

"Yes. They were passing through the wood. I went to fetch water and they tried to kill me but I ran."

"Shame they didn't catch you," Bart grumbled in his bowl.

Judith shot him a glare.

"Did they harm you?" Gertrude asked.

"No. They wanted my possession, so I gave them all I had."

"I'm sure you gave them that and more," her father-in-law chuckled.

"What did they look like?" Sam asked.

"They were ugly dog-faced men, with fat bellies and rusty daggers," she answered.

Sam's eyes grew wide and pottage dribbled down his chin.

"That's a fine dress you're wearing, Judith," her mother-in-law observed.

"It was given to me by a stranger in the wood. The bandits took my clothing."

"It will fetch a fine shilling in the market. Hurry and take it off, so we can sell it."

"I would like to keep it."

"Nonsense! That will pay for our food and more. Take it off."

Judith swallowed her anger and left the table to change.

She climbed up to the loft that reeked of molded hay.

As she untied the lace bodice of the dress, silent tears trickled down her cheeks. Why had she chosen to return? Was it because she could not face the baron, or face the truth of what she had done?

The truth seemed less frightening as she stood in the barren loft. The baron might have been angry with her, but she would have rather faced his anger, or lived a life in servitude, or died in a dungeon cell rather than live in servitude to the Timbolt family. She wished she would have run away from Caldwell, perhaps to another town, but the thought of her son drew her home. She could not bear to leave Sam.

She laid the beautiful dress aside and changed into one of her old dresses, quickly reacquainting herself with the discomfort of the scratchy wool.

Climbing back down from the loft, she was greeted by a table with dirty bowls left for her to clean. She tended to them and then took the leftovers to the pigs.

They grunted and snorted as they feasted on the molded bread, stale pottage and rotting vegetables. She covered her mouth as the scent of defecation gagged her.

She wandered away from the pigsty and saw her husband chopping firewood.

He held the axe in mid-air when she approached as if he expected her to say something. She wondered if he really cared about her safe return.

"Judith, I've been meaning to speak to you."

"Yes?"

"They found a woman's body in the woods, near the stream. Everyone thought it was you at first, since you had gone missing. She was wearing your dress. But it was not you; she was beautiful, a true flawless maiden. How did she get your dress? Did you... kill her?"

Insulted, Judith stammered, "K-kill her? How can you think I could be capable of killing anyone? It must have been a dress similar to mine."

"She wore *your* dress. I know it was your dress, the stains were the same."

Heat burned her cheeks. "I told you, I know nothing. My clothing was stolen. Your mother is going to have a fit if I don't get back to my chores."

He sighed. "Fine. Go, then."

She fled to the house, her nerves strung tight. Perhaps the truth was going to be as difficult as the lie.

That afternoon, Judith stood over the hearth stirring the large pot of stew. She rubbed the sweat off her forehead with her sleeve and looked towards the front door, hearing a commotion outside.

Her mother-in-law, standing beside her, threw her knife down. "What is going on out there?"

Judith watched her waddle to the window and peer out with a skeptical eye. Her back straitened and her jaw dropped. "Bless my eyes. It's Baron Blacwin."

Judith dropped the spoon into the stew.

She ran up next to Gertrude and peeked out the window for confirmation.

"What is he doing here?" Judith asked in horror.

"I don't know, but you better hurry up and get the table set for him!"

She peered out again to see Roger and personal guard with the baron.

Her head spun. "We're not having him in, are we?"

"Are you daft, child? Get that table set."

She watched in distress as her mother-in-law joined Garreth and his father to greet the baron. They kissed his ringed fingers and begged him to come inside. She prayed he would deny their request.

To her dismay, she heard him agree and they all headed for the door.

Judith was fear stricken and her heart begged fight or flight.

Flight won and she scrambled up the ladder to the loft. She backed into the corner, biting down on her knuckles and praying this was all a nightmare.

"Baron Blacwin, we insist you share our table," Garreth urged.

"Thank you," she heard the baron reply. "but, I do not wish to intrude. I just have some questions for you. It will only take a moment."

"Intrude? Nonsense," Gertrude said. "We will get you a nice bowl of stew. Judith! Where has your wife gone, Garreth?"

Judith cursed them all and slid down the wall to her knees, hiding her head in her hands. If only she could climb out of the window and escape. She knew her legs would break from the fall.

The ladder shook.

Someone was coming for her.

"Mummy? Are you up here?" Sam's head of marigold hair popped up to greet her. "Mummy, there you are! Baron Blacwin is here!"

"I don't care. Shush now and get back down stairs."

Confusion filled his big hazel eyes. "But Mummy, he has a big black carriage and a horse and a big feather in his hat! Don't you want to meet him?"

"No. Now go. I am not feeling well."

"Judith!" Gertrude yelled. "I need help serving the stew!"

"I cannot go down there. Please Sam, tell her I am ill."

"Come on Mummy, don't be scared. He is not frightful. He's not a bat."

"I know he isn't a bat!" she said, trying to wrangle her emotions of excitement and utter terror.

"Judith, get down here, you worthless witch!" Bart yelled.

Judith swallowed hard. What would happen if she *didn't* go down might be worse than facing the baron. Perhaps he would not recognize her in her drab rags.

"Better come Mummy," Sam said, frowning at her.

Reluctantly she stood up and followed Sam down the ladder.

"Good eve," she whispered with a bow, keeping her gaze to the ground.

She crossed the room to the hearth. Her hands shook as she ladled stew into each bowl.

She served the baron first, resisting the urge to look at him. When he took the bowl from her, their hands brushed. Everything in the room faded away as their eyes met. His lips parted in surprise. Dread crept over her. He recognized her.

Before he could speak, her mother-in-law interrupted.

"Are you going to stand there and stare at him all day, Judith? There are other hungry people at this table, too!"

She backed away and went to get the other bowls of stew.

She could feel his eyes on her as she ladled the stew and served the others at the table.

Sam dunked a handful of bread into his stew and chomped on it, looking up at the baron admiringly. "I like your feather."

"Thank you," the baron replied.

"My mummy collects bird feathers for me when she goes to the forest to find berries. She was kidnapped by bandits and she just came back home."

Judith winced and walked back over to the stew pot.

"Is that so?" the baron asked in a skeptical tone.

"She got lost and ran into bandits," Garreth added. "She is lucky to be alive. Isn't that so Judith?"

"Yes," she whispered without turning around.

"They were fat bandits with big swords," Sam added.

"Very interesting," Baron Blacwin answered.

Judith wished she could flee out the front door and never return.

"Mummy, tell him the story."

"I don't want to."

"I'd like to hear it, if you don't mind," Baron Blacwin said, his voice as smooth as silk.

Judith slowly turned around and looked over at the table, her eyes finally settling on him.

He leaned forward, his lips pulled tight in displeasure. "I'm sure it was a dreadful experience."

"It was humbling."

Her eyes pleaded with him.

"These bandits, did they assault you?" he asked, ignoring her distress.

"No, I ran," she answered, on the brink of tears.

"You ran, did you?"

"She ran, all right!" Bart chuckled. "Don't believe a word that comes out of her lying' lips, Baron. I'm sure she enjoyed whatever torture they gave her. Refill my ale, wench."

Judith obediently grabbed the ale pitcher and carried it to her father-in-law. She gripped the handle tightly in fear of spilling. As she drew it back, her unsteady grasp caused her to spill some down the back of her father-in-law's hand.

"Wasteful, stupid girl!" Bart threw his fist up, backhanding her across the face.

She stumbled back, dousing ale all over the floor as she fell into a pile of chopped firewood.

"Foolish child! Look what you have done!" Gertrude yelled.

She heard nothing but the ringing in her ears. Fiery pain seared her backside where she landed on the logs.

A teary blur came into view over her. The Baron. He held his hand out to her and pulled her to her feet.

She stood up, shaking, and looked at her son, pressed against his father's shoulder in fear.

Her husband, the coward, bowed his head in shame.

"What the hell is going on here?" the baron whispered against her ear.

"Thank you, Baron," Judith said, pulling out of his hold. She went to fetch a rag to sop up the ale from the floor. As she knelt down over the mess, she found it hard to hold back the tears.

"She is ignorant, my lord," her mother-in-law said.

The Baron was obviously disturbed. "It's fine. I need a private word with Judith regarding her disappearance."

"She is fine now," Garreth said, "Don't bother yourself, Lord Blacwin. I'm sure you have much more important things to worry about."

"I have a berry pie waiting," Gertrude said, enticingly.

"I have no need for dessert. Thank you," he answered in a cold voice.

"Judith, get the baron's cloak," her father-in-law said, bowing his head.

Judith wiped her tears away and went to retrieve the baron's cloak. She followed him to the door and looked up into his eyes, guilt stricken.

"Forgive me," she whispered.

"Come outside," he replied, holding the door open.

She stepped out obediently. Judith knew her family would be at the window listening, so she led him to the opposite side of the carriage.

The baron ordered his men to step aside until he was finished speaking with her.

Once everyone was out of sight, Judith wrapped her arms around him and buried her face into his black doublet.

"Forgive me, please. I meant you no harm, I swear to you." She sobbed.

He ripped her off him and stared into her eyes with distain. "What the hell is going on here? Who are you, truly?"

She took a deep breath. "My name is Judith Timbolt."

"Why have you deceived me?"

"I did not mean to. I just wanted to escape this life." Tears flowed down her cheeks and dripped from her chin.

"Where is the true Lora Noire?"

Tears obscured her vision of his face. "She is dead, my lord. I found her dead in the forest and I took her clothes. She poisoned herself."

"You found her dead? This is preposterous. You expect me to believe you did not take her life?"

"Yes! I swear to you I did not. I found her dead."

"You assumed her identity. You might as well have killed her."

"I did no such thing. I found her face down near the stream when I went to fetch water. I only wanted her dress but then a man came and he assumed I was her. He brought me to you... I didn't know what else to do!"

"Why did she kill herself?"

"Because she was being forced to marry you."

He looked surprised by that revelation and looked away, his jaw tightening.

"I wanted to marry you," she pleaded.

"Everything you told me was a lie," he scoffed. "You wound me deeply."

"You must find it in your heart to forgive me, please! I cannot live with myself otherwise."

"Forgive you? You do not deserve forgiveness. Do you know what you have done?"

His words pierced her. "I do, and I am sorry. I wanted to tell you, but there was no way, so I ran."

"This is treasonous!" he snapped. "What do I tell her father?"

"Tell him she killed herself. She is dead."

"She's more than dead. She's an imposter!" He looked off into the distance.

"I'm so sorry, Cal." She clutched at the front of his doublet again.

He tore her hands away. "Does your family know what you have done?"

She shook her head. "They know only what they told you."

He moved away from her. "I would reveal you, if it did not make me look the fool."

"Don't leave me here," she begged, her remorse becoming too much to bare.

"Where do you want me to take you?"

"Anywhere but here. Please!"

"You don't deserve to be saved after what you have done. I gave you enough," he said, his eyes cold.

She lowered her head into her hands and sobbed.

"Ready the carriage. I am through!" he yelled to his men.

"Baron Blacwin, please!" she called, reaching for him in a last attempt. "Don't you see why I am bruised? Why I ran?"

He glared down at her. "All I see is a liar who made a fool of me. Good day."

"She left a note!" Judith yelled. "She said that if she had to marry you then she would rather give herself to God than to be your baroness. She drank poison!"

His jaw tightened. "Quiet yourself!"

"No! You must believe me. You must!"

He took her by the shoulders and straightened her. "Stop this. You're making a fool of both of us."

"I don't care...I love you!" she wept.

A look of disgust crossed his face. "You love no one but yourself."

Sobs wracked her body. "Cal, please."

"Do not use my name, peasant." he let her drop to her knees before him.

Her lower lip trembled as she grabbed his knee, and looked up at him with pleading eyes.

"I am still the the woman you knew!"

"The woman I knew never existed!" He pulled away from her grip and stepped into his carriage.

She watched helplessly as he took one last look at her through the small window before drawing the curtain closed.

The reins snapped, the carriage lurched forward and rolled down the muddy road.

Judith pressed her forehead into her knees and wept.

Chapter 5

Two Months Later

Fall always arrived early in Caldwell, and the harvest kept the Timbolt family busy.

Judith maintained the house as she always did, busying herself with making jams, ciders, and non-perishables for the winter.

On an unpleasantly cold afternoon, Judith sat at the dining table with a basket of apples. She carefully peeled the mottled red skin from each one, readying them to dry for cider.

Samuel's soft laughter carried in through the open doorway as he played in a dry leaf pile.

A raucous cough broke the calm in the room. Her mother-in-law barreled through the front door with a basket of eggs, covering her mouth with her hand.

"Two of our laying hens froze to death last night and our milk pail has a hole. Finish those apples," she told Judith between deep breaths, "and go into town, I hear Henry had an overstock of chicks last spring."

Henry was the hunchback chicken farmer and town cooper.

"I'll need the cart for all of that. Is Garreth finished shoeing the horse?" Judith asked.

"He should be," Gertrude said, setting the basket of eggs down on the table and waddling back outside.

Judith finished peeling the apples and put them aside. She glanced over near the hearth where Garreth's hound lay asleep. She succumbed to a yawn wishing she could curl up beside him and sleep the rest of the day away.

She tied her woolen cloak around her shoulders and stepped out into the brisk autumn air to see Garreth waiting for her with the horse and cart.

"I won't be gone long," she said as he helped her into the seat.

"You're sure you don't want me to come along?"

"I will be fine."

He reached out and gave abdomen a soft rub. "I cannot believe we will have another mouth to feed next spring."

"If I carry well through the winter."

He took her hand. "Maybe we will have our home by then."

She pulled her hand away. "I will return soon."

She snapped the reigns and headed for town.

The market was bustling with villagers. She made haste to the cooper. Another man was in front of her, placing an order for twenty cider kegs. Judith waited her turn, glad to be free of her chores for a time.

"What can I do for you, Judith?" Henry called to her when he was ready.

"I need a new bucket and two laying hens if you have them."

"I've got the hens but the bucket will take a while. I have six orders to fill. Can you pick it up tomorrow evening?"

"Yes, that would be fine."

He nodded and marked down her order. "I hear you have a little one the way."

She smiled thinly and rested her hand over stomach. "Yes, next spring."

"Congratulations."

"Thank you."

He only asked payment for the chickens and gave her the bucket for free as a celebratory gift on her expectancy.

When she stepped out of the cooper's, she paused in the doorway as a black carriage barreled past her. She held her breath as it halted before the smith shop. Could it be the baron?

A scrawny man dressed in dark green climbed out of the carriage and hurried into the shop.

She carried the hen's cages to her cart and secured them in the back. She cast one last glance at the carriage with a heavy heart.

His warm hands, soft lips, and dark eyes carried her off to sleep each night. Her love for him was as real as his child that was growing in her womb.

Just as she was about to snap the reigns, a figure in a black cloak came out of the weapon shop. His back was to her, but she could never mistake his height or his posture. Her eyes watered as Baron Blacwin crossed in front of her, heading toward the armor shop across the road.

"Baron!" she called, nearly falling as she climbed out of the cart.

He did not hear her.

Her feet, clumsy with excitement, carried her toward the armor shop.

"Baron Blacwin!" she shouted in a last attempt.

The baron looked over expectantly with his hand on the door. His features hardened and he stared at her with scrutiny. "Judith."

She stood a good pace from him, unsure if she should approach.

"Baron Blacwin," she said with a curtsey.

He approached her and she lowered her gaze.

"How do you fare?" he asked.

"I have seen happier days. And you?"

"I, too, have been better."

She looked up at him again and his face blurred in her tears. "I was hoping you had forgiven me for my wrongs against you. I will never forgive myself. I am still so very sorry."

"Are you?"

"Yes, more than ever. I take it no one has captured your heart yet?"

"No one will captivate me like 'Lora Noire'." His voice dripped with sarcasm. "Though, as you know, she is dead, or never existed at all."

"She does exist and her heart is unchanged," she assured him.

"She belongs to another," he reminded her.

"Not her heart."

His eyes turned cold. "Hearts are weak and cannot be trusted. A good harvest to you, Judith Timbolt." He tipped his black hat to her and disappeared within the shop.

She bowed her head and walked back to the cart. It took all of her will to fight the tears building in her eyes. Would he ever find it in his heart to forgive her? Did it even matter?

Judith spent the next day making apple butter while her husband and father-in-law chopped a winter's worth of wood.

The smell of the roasting quail that Garreth had caught that morning caused her stomach to groan irritably. The pregnancy had been kind to her, besides giving her the appetite of a ravenous wolf.

When it came time for supper, she had only finished but three bites before she was dismissed from the table.

She had forgotten to retrieve the bucket from town. Her mother-in-law demanded she go fetch it.

Judith wearily walked to town, trying to ignore the emptiness gnawing in her stomach. To get her mind off her hunger pangs, she imagined what the child inside of her would become. Would he have the baron's dark eyes? His lips? His disposition? If only she could live with the baron and raise her children in the comfort she never knew, far away from the cold thatch house and Timbolt family.

When she reached town, most of the vendors were packing up their goods for the evening. Her heart sank when she saw that the bread merchant had left. She had hoped to beg for a stale loaf. Sighing, she continued to the cooper.

When she arrived, her bucket, smelling of fresh cedar, was waiting for her on the counter. She took it, thanked the cooper, and set back out onto the road.

Her stomach rumbled and she prayed there would be supper left at home when she returned.

The market square was empty besides two children chasing each other.

A merchant carrying a basket of apple passed before her. She could almost taste how sweet they were.

"Excuse me. Could I please make a purchase?" she asked, her mouth watering.

The man turned and looked her over with scrutiny. "How much ya got?"

"Three shillings." She grabbed at her pocket for the coins.

The sound of a horses hooves charging through the square drowned out the man's reply. A scream caught in her throat and she covered her head as a horse reared up behind her. The fruit merchant nearly dropped his basket.

She turned to see who tried to trample her, and looked into the eyes of the baron, seated on his snorting black steed. He tossed a satchel of shillings on the fruit-seller's basket.

"That should cover the cost of the basket."

Judith was speechless.

The merchant set the basket down beside her and took the coin.

"Thank you, my kind and gracious baron!" He backed away from them and hurried down the road.

She looked back to the baron, and he tipped his head. "Judith."

"That was overly generous of you."

"You looked hungry, and he was about to rob you of all you had."

"What are you doing here?"

"I was picking up my crossbow; it needed repairs."

"I see." She took an apple from the basket and rubbed it clean with her cloak. "I have no need for this whole basket of apples."

"Share it with your family."

"You are too generous. How could I ever repay you?"

"Might I have a moment alone with you?"

The apple that she was about to enjoy paused before her lips. "A moment alone?"

He offered his hand to her. "I don't have much time."

She contemplated his outstretched hand for a moment before she let him pull her up on the horse.

Blacwin nodded to his men on horseback across the road. "Bring this fruit to the Timbolt home at the edge of town! Call it a gift from the baron."

He snapped the reins and sent the horse jumping a step forward. She grasped his waist as they galloped out of the market.

Chapter 6

They rode down a forest path leading deep into thick woods. Her heart raced wildly in anticipation of where he might be taking her. She closed her eyes and clung to him, taking in his comforting scent as tree limbs scratched at her arms and stung her cheeks in passing.

When the horse slowed, Judith peeked around him to see ruins of an old church. The baron dismounted and reached up for her. She slid from the saddle into his arms. A cold breeze blew a lock of her hair into her eyes.

"What is this place?" she asked pulling away from him.

"It was once the first church of Caldwell."

"Why did you bring me here?" she asked wandering over to a crumbling wall and brushing some moss away to reveal a beautiful stained glass window.

"I have a question for you," he said, following her.

"Yes?"

He took her into his arms. "Do you wish to disappear for good, Judith?"

She furrowed her brows. "I...I don't understand."

His expression turned impatient. "You were so eager to leave everything behind when you took Lora's identity. So I ask you: Do you still wish to disappear?"

Fear consumed her and she took a step back. "You mean to execute me?"

"No, God, no," he shook his head. "I want to help you and your son get away from that family, if that is what you desire. I cannot forget the way he struck you. Knowing you are mistreated weighs on my mind."

"It does?"

He brushed his hand against her cheek. "Yes. I have not been able to forget you, no matter how hard I try. When I saw you in the market yesterday, I decided somehow I must help you."

She smiled and embraced him, placing her cheek against his chest. "You could take me as your wife."

"No, Judith." He pulled her back and looked into her eyes. "Let me explain what I have in mind."

She remained silent, waiting to hear what he had devised.

"We could feign your death. There are herbs that can make one fall into a deep sleep—so deep, it will be disguised as death itself. We can say it was self-inflicted. There are many ways. My point is, if they suspect your dead, you can find a new identity and flee Caldwell."

"It would be a selfless thing to do for me, but I cannot." She refused to leave Sam again.

"Why?" he asked.

"My son."

"I will find a way for him to be sent to you once you are safe."

"I don't see how any of this helps you in anyway."

He looked at her. "Knowing that you are well and no safe from harm will bring me peace."

"And you will take another for a wife?"

"If I were able to marry a peasant I would put a ring on your hand this very moment."

"What if I were carrying your unborn child in my womb?"

The sounds of the forest closed in on them. He studied her face, his dark eyes searching hers for meaning in her words.

"You are with child?"

Judith took his hand and pressed it firmly against her abdomen. "I am."

He blinked twice. "And it is… mine?"

"Yes, I am certain that it is. I cannot remember the last time I lay with Garreth."

"Does he suspect it's not his?"

"No. He cannot even recall the last time we lay together let alone what we had for supper last night."

"I do not know what to say," he said with a hint of elation. He leaned against a tree, rubbing his forehead.

"Do not say anything. Garreth is pleased; he knows no different."

"Yes, but I know different. He doesn't deserve you, or this child."

She grabbed his sleeve. "Then take us. Take what is willingly yours…"

He turned and took her by the wrist, his lips thin with irritation.

She held her breath, unsure of what he would do. When he pulled her against him and pressed a hard kiss against her mouth, her heart sang.

Their tongues danced and their hands caressed one another. When she pulled back to look into his eyes, she found a familiar the desire in them.

He bowed his head against her neck. 'I would take you now if I did not have the responsibility of a baron."

"I would gladly oblige," she whispered against his ear, lifting her leg against his waist.

His hand pulled her skirt back and caressed her naked thigh. "Judith, you belong to another. We should not."

"No my heart is yours," she pleaded, taking his face in her hands and kissing his lips again.

"It is a sin," he growled against her mouth, his hand trailing further up her leg.

"The sin is already made," she said, and placed his palm against her prominent abdomen.

They staggered into the ruined church and dropped to the ground. She settled on his lap and left reckless kisses on his lips while her hands fought his belt free from his trousers.

He unlaced her bodice and pulled her chemise down to expose her breasts. His tongue traced her taught nipples and made her whole body ache.

Her moans echoed through the dark wood and her hips burrowed down into him, aching for release.

Desire overcame the baron's conscience. He removed the last of her clothing and admired her, tracing his hand delicately over the proof of their previous indiscretion.

Their lovemaking had been different when she was Lora Noire. This time, there were no secrets and their feelings were sincere.

It was nearly sundown as they lay in each other's arms, wrapped in the warmth of his fur cloak. Not even the cold autumn air that whispered through the broken walls could cool the heat radiating between them.

Judith listened to his breathing and the excited beating of his heart, wishing there was a way she could be in his arms forever.

"If I go through with this plan, will you come see me after I am safe?"

"Of course I would," he assured her.

"Is there a chance I may not wake?"

"There's always a risk, Judith...just as there was when you claimed to be Lora."

She closed her eyes. "If I do not wake, will you make sure my son is well cared for?"

"Of course." He kissed her fingertips.

Before the woods became too dark to navigate, they redressed themselves and rode back out of the forest. They spoke of their plan to free her as they traveled back toward town.

Before long, the road that led to the Timbolt cottage came into view.

The baron dismounted and helped her to her feet.

She watched a hot plume of his breath escape his lips. "We will meet tonight, by the stream?"

"Yes, by the stream north of the cottage. It is in a clearing. I'll wait there for you there."

"Until then, Judith," he called out, re-mounting his horse.

He passed her the bucket, which he had carried on his saddle, and gave his horse a few swift kicks. She watched him gallop off into the darkness toward the manor.

She could not wipe the lighthearted smile off her face even when she stepped inside the cottage. She found her mother-in-law knitting in her rocking chair near the hearth.

"It's about time you returned home. We thought the bandits had taken you again."

"No, the bucket was not ready. I had to wait for it."

She seemed pleased with that response. "The baron sent us a basket of fruit."

"Did he? How kind of him."

"Everyone fell asleep waiting for you."

She could hear her father-in-law snoring in the first floor bedroom. Thankfully, she did not have to answer to him as to why she was late

She climbed up the ladder and dressed in her nightclothes, figuring she would rest until the hour came for her escape. She settled onto the straw pile next to her husband and son. Garreth mumbled a few slurred phrases. She pulled the thin blanket they shared over her body. Sam wrapped his small arm around her, and laid his head on her shoulder. She kissed his temple and tears burned her eyes.

This would be the last night she slept on coarse hay in the cold. It was her last night at Judith Timbolt.

The scenario of her escape danced repeatedly in her mind. She could see it, her husband weeping over her dead body, covered in animal blood. They would collect her lifeless form and mourn her. After she was placed in a coffin the baron would take her body-- and she would awaken a free woman.

She waited until the moon was high overhead before she redressed. Upon reaching the bottom of the ladder, she found Gertrude slumped over in her chair with a smoking pipe between her lips. A quiet snore escaped her as Judith crept past her. Pulling on her cloak, she took the small lantern near the door and cast her mother-in-law one last, worried glance before she escaped into the dark night.

The moonlight guided her along the road. She made her way to the stream and stood at the water's edge. The Baron had not arrived yet.

The stream glowed under the harvest moon. Her reflection on the water echoed her excitement. She recalled the last time she had stood at the stream, when she found Lora.

Dropping to her knees on the stiff, dry grass, she peered up at the night sky speckled with stars and wondered if she was making the right decision. She hated the thought of how her son would react when he found out she had died. Reuniting with him would be so sweet. She imagined their new life— a life free of misery. She might become a seamstress, she always liked sewing. Maybe she would have her own farm or even marry into a wealthy family. She decided that she would honor Lora by keeping her first name. Lora Cartwright. Cartwright was her maiden name and she missed it.

As the moments passed, it grew colder.

She wondered if the baron was going to help her after all.

What if he changed his mind?

She held back a scream when his leather-gloved hand clasped her shoulder and his warm breath traveled over her neck. "I hope I did not keep you waiting long."

A smile creased her lips. "I'd wait forever for you."

She turned to him and kissed him, savoring the warmth of his mouth against hers.

He gathered her into his arms and carried her to his horse. They rode along the path that led through the village of Caldwell and beyond.

A fog had settled onto the road, and suddenly the smell of fire choked her. It always brought her back to the fateful night she lost everything. Sadness filled her heart at the thought of some poor family's life going up in flame as hers had.

She clutched her heart as she realized the direction the smoke was coming from-- the Timbolt cottage.

Panic racked her body.

"Cal, the cottage is on fire!" She pointed to the orange light dancing between the trees in the distance, confirming her suspicion.

Cal gave his horse a few swift kicks and they galloped ahead.

When they rounded the bend, they found the home engulfed in black smoke and hot cinder.

"Sam!" she screamed, dropping from the horse and running to the front door.

"Judith, wait!" Baron Blacwin yelled behind her.

She ignored his pleas and threw herself through the front door.

Hot cinders blew into her eyes and smoke choked her. She held her sleeve over her mouth and nose, trying to hear her son crying.

Please, God, let him be alive, please!

She rushed to the ladder and screamed his name.

She heard a soft cry behind her and saw Sam crouched in the corner, holding his knees.

She ran to him and scooped his soot-covered body into her arms. Pulling her cloak over her shoulder, she held it against his nose and mouth.

She stumbled toward the door with him, feeling faint with relief when she saw Cal waiting for her. He reached his arms out to take Sam from her.

She passed him to the safety of the baron's arms, and something caught her leg.

She stifled a scream as she peered down at her father-in-law's bleeding face and his meaty fist gripping her ankle. He was crushed under a pile of burnt debris.

"Help me, witch!" he choked.

"Let me go!" she cried, afraid she might meet the same fate if she remained in the smoke-filled air.

"You'll burn in hell with the rest of us!"

Judith screamed as ceiling debris rained down around them and blocked her way to the door.

A spray of orange sparks ignited her cloak. Her heart could not possibly beat any harder as she swatted at the smoldering material attached to her neck.

It was becoming increasingly hard to breathe.

Smoke burned her eyes and filled her lungs, weakening her. She fell to the ground.

"Mummy!" Sam screamed from the doorway.

"Judith!" the baron yelled. "Get out of there!"

Bart's grip on her ankle was still firm. Too weak to fight, she feared she would not escape alive. A tear streaked her cheek as her son screamed to her from the doorway where the baron held him.

'I am so sorry, Sam,' was her last thought before the smoke consumed her.

The heat and smoke were gone, but she could still smell it. Her lashes parted slowly and sunlight scorched her eyes. Something warm brushed her cheek.

She jerked her face away, snapping her eyes shut. "No!"

"Judith, shh, you are safe," the baron said.

She peered up to see Baron Blacwin leaning over her, his dark eyes full of concern.

She blinked and looked around to make sure she was not dreaming…she was in his solar.

Was she dreaming?

So many questions sprung into her mind at once. The memory of her last moments in the fiery hell flooded her mind. Most important, where was Sam?

"Where is my son?" She sat up to see Sam sitting on the foot of the bed playing with some wooden toys, clean and content.

"Sam!" she cried holding her arms out to him.

"Mummy!" He leapt on her and wrapped his arms tightly about her neck. She breathed in relief and embraced him, kissing the top of his head. "Thank God."

"We have been waiting for you wake up, Mummy. I was scared you were dead, but Baron Blacwin promised me you would come back."

Judith glanced toward the baron who stood aside to let them reunite.

"Sam, why don't you go visit the puppies in the stable. I bet they miss you." The baron said.

Sam nodded enthusiastically. "They do. I named them all. You can come see them when you feel better Mummy."

"I will," Judith promised.

The baron smiled. "We can hear all about their clever names over supper. Go now."

Sam obeyed, pulling out of his mother's arms and walking to the door. He paused and peered over his shoulder at his mother again as if he could not believe she was there. He smiled and closed the door behind him.

"I do not know what to say," she said, wiping the tears from her face. "I owe you my life. Our lives."

"Rest for now. You can make it up to me when you are well."

"I'll do whatever you ask."

"Even become my baroness?"

Judith blinked in confusion. "Your baroness? You said—"

"I know what I said, Judith." He settled on the bed beside her and took her hand in his.

"I don't understand."

"I searched the town records this morning and I could not find any information on you other than your marriage to Garreth. All I would need to do is make a new public record for you, stating you are the daughter of a wealthy family, all of whom perished, and you married Garreth as a last resort. If that is not enough, you are carrying my heir."

Tears flooded her eyes. "Garreth…he died?"

"They all perished, besides you and Sam."

She looked down, feeling sudden unexpected remorse. She may not have loved Garreth the way a wife should, but she never wanted him to die.

"I understand if you need time to mourn. We do not have to speak of this again until you are ready."

She glanced up at him. "I cannot believe this. It's as if…"

"As if it was fate," he finished for her.

"Yes."

Tears spilled down her cheeks as she realized that she would never have to suffer another moment cold or hungry.

He leaned in and kissed her tears away. "It's over Judith."

She laughed in elation and wrapped her arms around his neck.

She had her son, the man she loved, and the promise of a beautiful tomorrow. It was more than she could have ever dreamed.

The End

About the Author

This is J.C. Murtagh's first published work and she has many more to share. She lives in Las Vegas, Nevada, with her husband and son.

For information on upcoming releases visit
http://www.JCMurtagh.com

www.ingramcontent.com/pod-product-compliance
Lightning Source LLC
Chambersburg PA
CBHW071204130626
46555CB00004B/1574